I WROTE STONE THE SELECTED POETRY OF RYSZARD KAPUŚCIŃSKI

The Selected Poetry of Ryszard Kapuściński

I WROTE STONE

Translated from the Polish
by Diana Kuprel and Marek Kusiba

BIBLIOASIS

Originally published in Poland as *Notes* by Czytelnik, Warsaw, in 1986 and as *Prawa natury* by Wydawnictwo Literackie, Kraków, 2006.

Cover and interior photographs by Ryszard Kapuściński

FIRST EDITION

LIBRARY AND ARCHIVES CANADA CATALOGUING IN PUBLICATION

Kapuściński, Ryszard
    I wrote stone / Ryszard Kapuściński; [translated by] Diana
    Kuprel, Marek Kusiba.

Poems translated from the Polish.
ISBN 978-1-897231-37-1

    I. Kuprel, Diana, 1963– II. Kusiba, Marek, 1951– III. Title.

PG7170.A58415 2007   891.8'518   C2007-904555-3

Edited by Daniel Wells and Stephen Henighan

PRINTED AND BOUND IN CANADA

In memory of Ryszard Kapuściński
4 March 1932 – 23 January 2007

CONTENTS

AT THE DOORWAY to Ryszard Kapuściński's Warsaw study is a pair of bast moccasins—their wide strips of inner bark woven into rough, thick soles, and cross-hatched to secure the feet. The moccasins were hand-crafted in Polesie, formerly one of Poland's eastern borderland provinces, where Kapuściński was born on March 4, 1932.

Until the Second World War, Kapuściński's family had lived in the town of Pińsk, a river port and important marketplace now in Belarus that was remarkable for its cultural, ethnic and linguistic diversity. After five months of Soviet occupation of eastern Poland, in February 1940, the Kapuścińskis, along with thousands of other refugees, fled this land of forests and rivers, of impenetrable swamps and peat-bogs. They made their way westward, to the environs of German-occupied Warsaw.

There the young Kapuściński experienced, first-hand, extreme deprivation and terror, and was eyewitness to round-ups and executions—subjects that would preoccupy him in his work as a journalist for over fifty years. His shabby, clumsy, wooden shoes would come to be, for him in those destitute years, a sign of abjectness, the mark of a person stripped of all dignity and sentenced to an inhuman existence. A symbolic artifact of the writer's origins, biographical and spiritual, then, the Poleskie bast moccasins seem an apt entrée to this English translation of his poetry.

Kapuściński is not known as a poet, and yet he never quit writing poetry. He is, rather, internationally acclaimed as a reporter who spent the last half of the twentieth century on the front lines, covering (by his own count) twenty-seven revolutions, rebellions and coups d'etat, who ranged and wrote across the Middle East, Africa and Latin America, who bore witness to the collapse of colonialism in the Third World and the crumbling Soviet Empire. He is the bestselling author of such classics of world literature as *The Emperor, Shah of Shahs, Imperium, Another Day of Life, The Soccer War, The Shadow of the Sun* and *Travels with Herodotus*— works that have been translated into over thirty languages and that have earned him numerous literary and journalistic awards, honorary degrees from universities around the world and fame as one of the most important writers of our time.

In 1986, when Kapuściński decided to publish *Notes* [Notebook], a slim collection of poems written over a period of almost forty years, it created a sensation among Polish critics. For two decades, this work, however, remained untranslated, but for a bilingual edition in Italian of his by then complete published poetry.

Yet a connection exists between his poetry and his larger body of work. There is the value Kapuściński ascribed to the art of poetry, and his belief that poetic discourse was able to illuminate dimensions of human experience that otherwise would remain unknowable. In an interview in 2005, he explained: "I cannot imagine that I would be able to write anything without first having read poetry. It is the highest form of language. . . . I believe that a poet is someone who preserves language and, for that reason, stands at the gates of its inexhaustible wealth, its simultaneous beauty and threat. I value poets and poetry because poetry is something more than a transmitter of information or a well-told story; it's a strange form which is comfortable in what is hidden right before our eyes, where, in a few stanzas, one can raise to a boil a powerful freight of experience and transgression at the same time. Poetry is the greatest alchemy of language because the poet concentrates on what is happening when words strike against themselves and new meanings arise—meanings thanks to which the world has a more comprehensive form, both visible and invisible."*

The significance of poetic discourse, for the writer, is evident in Kapuściński's grand reportage. He declares in the second volume of his *Lapidarium*, a collage of notes and citations written in 1972 and between 1980 and 2006: "I cannot forsake poetry. It requires that one attend profoundly to language, which is good for prose. Prose must have music, and poetry is rhythm. When I start writing, I must locate the rhythm. It carries me along like a river." His works of creative non-fiction are, in fact, remarkable for their breathtaking negotiation between the arts of journalism and belles lettres, for the author's ingenious ability to adapt his literary style to suit topic and context, such that what is described seems to come, organically, from inside a specific climate, culture or situation. Blending the objectivity of a reporter, the disposition of a historian and philosopher, the empathy of a humanitarian and the incantatory power of a poet, he transformed acts of incisive journalism into stunning—and significant—works of literature.

That Kapuściński should have practised poetry, then, is not surprising. He debuted as a writer in 1949 with a poem in a Polish literary weekly. Throughout his life, he continued to write poems in those moments when he found prose inadequate to express his thoughts.

True to his vocation, his ambition as a reporter was to cast light on worlds undergoing violent transformations. He considered himself, above all, an explorer of Otherness—of other cultures, other ways of thinking, other types of being. His mission was to come into contact with strangeness in order to understand it. For this, personal presence was crucial: he was the hero of his own books, as he declared in *Lapidarium II*, because they describe a person who travels, looks around, reads, reflects and writes.

Poetry, then, offers a new take on the Kapuścińskian mission. What he found in poetry was a means of exploring those regions in the human that may otherwise be forever left unexamined. Inspired by his extensive travels, meetings and observations, the poems complement his reportages: the external journeys to faraway places become recast through the poetic form into a journey of the human spirit.

The title of his first volume, *Notes* [Notebook], signals that his poems are a special kind of dispatch—a dispatch from an inner experience that synthesizes, cleanses, fulfills. The poems inquire into the essence of being human, and allude to the spiritual wasteland that is the human condition. They constitute an attempt to locate the individual within the crowd, and examine and confront what the author considered to be a frightful sickness: indifference.

His second volume, *Prawa natury* [The Laws of Nature], was published in 2006, two decades after *Notes*. The poems, employing a fragmentary poetic, reveal Kapuściński's private self as he grappled with the loss of friends and with his own physical vulnerability and mortality. Here he probes a profound loneliness that is, for him, the inability to connect with others.

His poetry, so sparing in expression, so simple and transparent, but also melancholic and impassioned, enters the most humanitarian current in the Polish lyric. While he is sensitive to poetry's magic, he expresses at the same time a suspicion about the nature of language, hardly surprising for someone who lived under the yoke of Communism. Perhaps for this reason his writing is a study in restraint and abbreviation.

Kapuściński was readying himself for a trip to Polesie, which was to be the subject of a future book, when, in December 2006, he was admitted to hospital to undergo cancer surgery. He passed away in Warsaw on January 23, 2007 after succumbing to a heart attack. He was 74.

—Diana Kuprel and Marek Kusiba

---

* From Wojciech Kass's interview with Ryszard Kapuściński, "Przeciw odmetaforyzowaniu języka" [Against the de-metaphorization of language] in *Nowa Okolica Poetów* 1/2005.

Some of the figures and writers to whom Kapuściński dedicated, or referred, in his poems:

Jerzy Popiełuszko (J.P.) (1947–1984), Catholic priest from Poland associated with the Solidarity movement who was murdered by the Communist secret police.

Arnold Słucki (1920–1972), Polish poet and publicist.

Konstantin Biebl (1898–1951), Czech poet.

Tadeusz Nowak (1930–1991), Polish poet and writer.

Edward Stachura (1937–1979), Polish poet and prose writer.

James Dickey (1923–1997), American poet and novelist.

NOTEBOOK

TATARS' WASTELAND

They left behind sawdust and stalks
yellowed grass dried-up bush
cracked earth empty wells
rock piles cold wind
just bone and junk
and mould and dust
the tetter of rust
and silence
    interrupted from time to time
by an iron clamour and a barked command

A Summation

Battered faces
busted spines
CVs rewritten
shredded
not required

Barbed Wire

You write about the man in the camp
I write about the camp in the man
for you barbed wire is outside
for me it rankles the insides of each of us

—You really think there's a big difference?
These are just two sides of the same torment

People at the Bus Stop on Wolska Street

Misery
misery
in the evening
misery's drunk

Cancer

Worry lines
bent inward
dark substances
find no outlet

Pain

Under siege the body crucified
a tear seeks a way
along furrows in the face
perhaps it can deliver itself
from this hell

Autumn in the Park

Such a crimsoning that
in a moment fire
of gold and ochre that
just-just Sahara
and yet chill
and instead of Hosanna
rustle
a tread

time withdraws

Snow

Walking to the swish-song of boots
a sudden ray of sun
fleeing the clouds
whiteflashes into a bird

ECOLOGY

And once we are stuck in the ruts of the Polish road
once we are mired in the sands of history
and horses whipped on by our dreams
are unable to take even one more step
do not curse heaven or earth
do not damn the world or fate

look
a bird soars
the forest rustles

a dung beetle, cockchafer and ladybug
crawl along a path

LANGUAGE

Leaving for Warsaw
he told me not to worry
I'll keep you in mind
I just have to figure out what and how

after a year he wrote
to come
something's in the works

he had an office with an eagle on the wall
highly polished etcetera

Miss Bożenka brought in two coffees
two Georgian cognacs
it's good for this weather

the day was chilly, dripping
people at the bus stop buried their heads and hid themselves

you can start tomorrow
nothing great, he admitted
but your foot is in

just watch it
here it's slippery going
one false step and you're flat
experts only

his laugh was not jolly

then we'll bring Henry and Władek on board
decent guys who deserve a life
when there's more of us we'll make our way
we'll just have to kick that one over
he pointed at someone behind the wall
his face darkened

it was obvious that one still had power
he could still take us down

that's why I began my wrestling lessons
right off
ho ho, he chortled
no fear you'll be disqualified
for stalling on the mat

SCULPTOR FROM ASHANTI

In the trunk of a teak tree
he seeks a pair of eyes

he hews and chisels away the first layer
uncovers nothing
ever more impatient
he bores

but sees nothing beneath the barked eyelid
he peels back
no pupil

close to the pith
he comes upon a pair of eyes

he looks
terror-struck

ON EXHIBIT:
"PHOTOGRAPHS OF POLISH PEASANTS PRIOR TO 1944"

I gaze upon you,
grandmother,
as you sit so
in stiff lace,
a long skirt,
in front of the hut in Rakocice
—the date beneath the photo
1913.

You don't know yet
what I've long known:
in a year everything will shudder,
armies will mount.

But for now it's quiet here,
not many people.
I overhear
one girl say to another
—the one in the Austrian uniform
is the spitting image of Bogdan.

in Africa there are nights so black that standing in the midst of darkness we sense the whole world vanish, fallen into the maw of Hades

yet how wrong we are: shine a lantern and on the threshold of darkness a herd of elephants watch warily

if next we cast a ray to the left or right, we plunge the elephants into darkness again and in the grass discover the maned lions circling uneasily, awaiting the dawn and their time to feed

farther on, timorous giraffes run from even this weak light for fear it will wound them deeply

and here crowd the nimble antelope, sluggish but dangerous water buffalo, hippopotami sunk in mud, unruly baboons—everything sleeps as a mouse upon a box sleeps and yet does not for each fears the other; all around predators lurk so that should the defenceless zebra or quaking kid doze instantly would they feel fangs sink into their necks

we rub our eyes and marvel at the lifeless-seeming dark, for we have not even mentioned the colourful, silver-voiced birds, sly, poisonous reptiles, disgusting toads, exquisite butterflies

and what of the tireless bustle of termites? the intrepid scarabaeus prodding a wheel of fresh dung?

the trees and shrubbery and herbs? the bougainvillea flower whose scent reminds us that it is here and sleeps not? the vines curling patiently upward?

when the lantern fails, darkness falls again, but a
moment later from out of the deep dusk a pair of human
eyes emerge—the eyes of a native, but who? an honest
herder, an enigmatic witch doctor or—God forbid—an
assassin from Bokassa's guard? the eyes approach and oh
wonder! they're the eyes of an African girl, in her hair a star

I resolved to withdraw because I was becoming worse for people.

It's not that I was wronging them deliberately or that I consciously wanted to hurt them.

I was worse in that I was growing more indifferent to them and my indifference was disillusioning them.

I was no longer able to reciprocate their feelings, I even treated them as irrelevant, a burden.

The other came to represent a constraint, a chokehold, paralysis, his presence agitated me, suffocated, I had to flee in order just to draw a breath. That is why I cast off everyone.

In this I saw my salvation.

I don't know if I'll end up in the monastery cell, a forest retreat or some other seclusion, maybe I'll have to create a hermitage in myself, raise up the walls inside, slam the gates shut.

It's a weakness, a betrayal even, I know, but I no longer have the strength to carry anyone, I cannot do as St. Christopher, I'm not able to bear you across the river.

All in me that had to do with the other refused my bidding.

CUDGEL

in memoriam to J.P.

1

. . . when contriving methods of killing
various techniques are considered

2

yet one always comes back to the simplest
(to the dismay of technocrats
convinced only their goddesses exist)
a cudgel will do—
a gnarled branch

3

tree:
potential armoury for instruments of torture and murder

4

and we struggle so to preserve the forests
forgetting that
while on the face of this earth
but one tree remains
people will die by the wooden cudgel

5

pegs
jabbed under the nail
of the earth

CLOUD

Primordial creature
in perpetual search
of shape and place

some extol prayers for its coming
others entreat it to be gone

always under pressure of contradictory desires

hence the wandering
about the sky
the hesitation

where to take refuge

Whosoever creates his own world will live on.
God lives—He created His own world,
Homer lives, and Michelangelo and Mozart.
Raphael created myriad figures—they all live.

Hieronymus Bosch's monstrosities seethe.
Renoir's women display their flesh—beautiful.
Chagall's roosters crow, his calves gambol about the sky.
Don Quixote mends his arms, Sancho Panza philosophizes
    still.

How many more worlds will arise?
How many characters?
How many animals?

A second Noah's Ark?

LASH

Person 1:

    You must stand up
    to what surrounds you
    you must be here
    but be
    otherwise
    you must learn what is singularity
        and that it be
    not arrogance but strength

Person 2:

    You must and you must
    like the whistle of a lash

THE POET ARNOLD SŁUCKI ON NEW WORLD STREET

Before leaving
for Jerusalem
he would stroll down New World Street
he would look without seeing anyone
an old coat without a single button
his forehead always sweated

his pockets full of poems

He took out one after the other

In the doorway
touching my arm
he asked me to read

Good?
Not good

Heart-broken
he pulled out the next
five, ten

In the end he pulled out a pigeon

And what is that? I asked

Don't you see?
My last poem!
Did you not know a bird is a poem?
Poetry wing-borne?

One of them
writes a poem
and sends it out into the world
a second does the same
and a third

Poems encounter one another
stand for hours on street corners
they don't notice night fall
that it's begun to rain

Perhaps it's insomnia
thinks a drenched passerby
perhaps they've nowhere to go
in such a downpour

Biebl:
the sea deforms the response of the drowned

ALREADY

Already we watch for you always
already we prepare food and drink
already the hut is clean, the windows are like mirrors
already the gate is garlanded in flowers and spruce

Already Mercury and Venus prophesy you
soothsayers presage your imminent arrival
they burn incense and pay homage
at night they keep vigil, prepare for matins

But you show up unnoticed
you have neither crown nor wings
you are neither princess nor archangel

just the strongest beating of the heart

THEY

They sit
facing one another

she thinks
what a great guy

they drink

outside it's dark
evening surrounds the town
occupies the streets
drives out the pedestrians

suddenly
he reaches inside himself
pulls out a toad

she looks
doesn't believe her eyes

he pulls out cockroaches
a whole handful
octopi, polyps
spiders
crawl out on their own accord
creep

he hurries
there's still
more

a tramp's stinky clogs
a bag lady's putrid sack
filthy midgets
vampires
hags

the table at which they sit
(still life with empty bottle)
comes to life

the toad croaks
the cockroaches crawl
the spiders swell with venom

in the poisoned mist
he flounders
stammers

with what remains of his strength
he trundles outside

and disappears

dragging his feet

A DREAM

I see an iceberg, boreal solitude,
the Arctic Ocean, I suspect,
the Far North anyway,
the pole perhaps.

Clouds are strewn,
heavy, bouldered fields
in a dejected,
lightless sky.

The berg, tall and steep,
flows imperceptibly along the sea
in a still vastness
that is its own kind of absolute.

I see people on its slopes.
Strange, why are they here
in this desert fettered
by a crashing frost?

Could they be castaways from the Titanic?

I see them struggle
while an inexplicable force
bears steadily downward,
their raw fingers grasping at the glassy hulk.

This is their here and now.

I see their swollen hands,
grey faces, anguish and pain.
I see their strength trickling away.
They lose balance.
If one slips,
all the ranks tumble down

—a terrifying pantomime
these wracked bodies.

Now
a voice reaches me.
Someone's calling for perseverance
and as *memento*
points at the sea,
and I see their petrified glances,
and I know their consciousness is paralyzed
even more than their frozen bodies.
They're possessed of that thought after which
no other is possible,
no humanity.
They tell themselves,
our torment, our drudgery is not so terrible,
somehow we will adapt
so long as it will not get worse.

Then I began to study them,
the beggared ones,
their clothing ripped by the graupel gales,
the condemned, starving wretches
were in their own way content.

They hug the glacial cliffs
with a kind of joy
and regard the iceberg
with a shadow of pride
for they've grown fond of their lot.

In a sudden blizzard burst
I lost sight of the iceberg
and alone in this stony solitude I realized,
one should weep for human misery,
the cruel, boundless misery of man,
misery of the heart and mind,
misery of sight and sound,
misery of arms and legs,
misery our own and others',
misery evil and blind,
misery of fate,
unfathomable,
immeasurable
misery of existence.

Misery of God.

RAVENS

When they enter upon this road
they hurry but just as time flows
the frames of film advance more slowly:
more and more crosses by the road

there are birds too
I admire the ravens
their sullen majesty

A CONVERSATION WITH J.

I asked
if A. committed suicide

I wouldn't say that
he replied
it was a leave-taking

A. withdrew slowly
it went on for some time
at first he showed up less and less often
he disappeared
lost touch

at first
you don't pay much attention

once I met him on the street
here
he said, tapping his head
I have nothing here

he walked off
bent over
as if sewn up in a sack

he told someone
that what he sees
gets smaller and smaller
it shrivels
then shatters

there remained only
scattered points in space

for awhile
they would whirl about in the air
like snowflakes
until they disappeared

the world began to sink
into non-being

he followed

YOGI RAMAMURTI

Yogi Ramamurti bids
he be buried in a grave
he will remain there one week
doctors will testify it's not a scam

whoever wishes can go down the tunnel
watch through a window:
Ramamurti lies in a grave
not breathing

everyone is asked for a donation
the buried one wants to earn money
that's why he went to the grave:
to survive

after a week they dig up the yogi
Ramamurti emerges
weakened
he's touched the absolute
that's always exhausting

he bows to the gathering
counts the donations
102 rupees
less than ten dollars

everyone disperses
an empty grave remains

Ramamurti was reborn
but he's still a beggar

weeks pass
he has nothing to eat
he's dying of hunger

I'm going back to the grave
he says
only in death
life

Professor Kant
strolling along his beloved Lorenzstrasse
at a certain point breaks off his walk
and quickly returns home

It's not the rain
so frequent in Königsberg this time of year
but an insight
he wishes urgently to jot down:

the human being is not a thing
act so that you treat humanity, whether in your own person or
in that of another, always as an end, never as a means only

He tracks the bird in flight
this is the instant he forgets about everything
caught up

Please watch out, Professor,
the sidewalk is slippery
please do not rush so

St. Augustine:
afterward I again fell towards the things of this earth, weeping.

Ah yes

it took a long time
before I learned to think about man
as a human being
before I discovered this way of thinking
before I took this path
in this salutary direction
and speaking of man or contemplating him
I stopped asking such questions as
is he white or black
an anarchist or monarchist
fashionable or outmoded
ours or theirs
and I began to ask
what in him is of human being

and is he

and I also asked whether to be a human being is a given,
it happens of its own accord, or whether one must bear
steadily toward it, acquiesce to it faithfully, awaken in
oneself the desire to be a human being

and henceforth I began to look for him
in his distinctiveness
in his uniqueness
I wanted to draw near
above all to the human being in myself
inside my own self

I desired that he exist in me
without labels, signs, banners
without a tomahawk
or plumes

that he cast away his tin bugle

*

The elderly gent
holds up
his spittled finger

checks which way
the wind is blowing

then
positions himself accordingly
and flies off

not high
not far

A CHOICE

To walk away
to slam the lid of silence
or yet again
to take up the effort anew

to free the throat from the stranglehold
to fight to breathe
to pronounce a word
to utter a whole sentence
to speak up
in haste
before they once again apply the gag

I know you're waiting
you
who listen intently
who put your ear
to a deaf wall

*

To locate the true word
which is in its prime
is calm
breaks not into hysterics
has no fever
experiences no depression

it can be trusted

to locate the pure word
which didn't slander
didn't snitch
didn't take part in a raid
didn't declare black white

one can hope

to locate the wingéd words
which would allow one
be it by just a fraction of an inch
to lift oneself above this all

*

Why
did the world
fly past me
so quickly

it did not let itself be held
approached
addressed in the familiar

it pursued
the vanishing point
in fire and smoke

THE LAWS OF NATURE

*

Perhaps the greatest thing
expresses itself with silence
like the universe

the word
an appearance
an attempt to grasp
the ungraspable

the suspicion that words
erect false signposts
lead one to dead ends
lead one into temptation

THE LAWS OF NATURE

In this place
the earth gives way
forms a valley
along its bottom a river runs

a narrow current
seeks a great water
visible even on school maps
it would immerse itself in the abyss
vanish into verdant depths

it becomes an ocean
dangerous, unfordable
engulfs the daredevil, madman, castaway
wipes them from the restlessly undulating surface

what remains are the very laws of nature
after life—death
at the end of a sunlit valley
Styx and icy murk

and another river drowns
in the ocean chasm

I WROTE STONE

I wrote stone
I wrote house
I wrote town

I shattered the stone
I demolished the house
I obliterated the town

the page traces the struggles
between creation
and annihilation

DISCOVERIES

Pain bursts your heart:
you begin to sense the heart

your eyes suddenly go blind:
you begin to sense the eyes

your memory drowns in darkness:
you begin to sense memory

you discover yourself
through the denial of the self

you exist
through the negation of existence

*

From the recesses of memory
shades emerge,
they roam the streets,
cross the town square,
their silhouettes vague,
unable to stay anyone,
say a word.

Sometimes they lift their faces,
visible briefly in the bled light
of a distant even lost recollection,
their features marred and crackled
—it's an effort to put names to them.

The final experience of life
is always painful,
either lengthy and brave
or sudden,
a piece of lead in the back of the head.

After a time
they show up on the square,
then disappear around the corner.

Let's summon them all,
no, not the roll of a drum or a call
but an encounter, an
"it's good that you are,
you disappeared for so long,
I can't believe you were all that busy."

Yesterday a weary Christ came to me
in a dream and said,
"It's gotten so it's hard to get
a glass of clean water."

I know that when you're far away
I feel it every night,
my body shifts about in the emptiness
"On a bed of gravel".*

Obscure cosmic events
created a planet so vast
that I can see but not touch you.
If the cosmos were comprised of planets
small like a grain of sand,
we could like a fleck of dust
vanish in the sun.

To exist in purgatory,
circulating between those who've passed away
and the keepers of their memory,
delivering letters, smuggled notes, dispatches,
signals,
passwords,
glances.

Nothing so unites people
as death.

Contemplating St. Theresa of Avila
we begin to comprehend what is God:
God is exultation.
If your wings are folded or clipped
you will not draw nigh.

* From James Dickey's poem, "A Folk Singer of the Thirties,"
  in *Helmets*

Saturday night
in this town
does not sleep

Along the main street
tires hum, raised voices
pass beneath the window
in arguments elated and banal

Unable to sleep
I read the paper:
heart attacks claim their victims most often
between 8 and 9 A.M.

It's 2:15

*

A leaf
torn from its limb
shivers, shakes
it quiets itself only
when it touches the ground

BRITRAIL TO WALES

Through the window the leas, trees
untiring rivers
the kingdom of silence and patience
welcomes you should you take the step
England green on both sides of the rail
the cars lull each of us
confined to our own destinies

Evesham
come back
will you?
waiting—a thorny dream
my world acquired a new dimension
from here on I am other
the earth upon which I tread
is other

A horse, then three, one stock-still
now up and up the scape
soars and arches

In Monmouth copper cobbled (copper beech)
a grand tree
looked at from a distance a reddish gold
close up it changes to green

for a second I cannot descry the beauty
I am not able to focus

GEOGRAPHY

The road
once walked
vanishes behind you
ceases to exist

geography—a subjective concept
a kind of agreement

*

Roots have verticality
they descend into the earth
they bore down deep
their being invisible, dark
they strain to push aside grains of sand
stones, rock
to push through lava and mineral
cast up to the surface
idle
they wither
their knotted fingers stretched to the heavens
their prayer confused and untranslatable

the knowledge of roots:
life comes from penetrating depth

ROSARY

of wood
of bone
of glass
ten after ten
strung
knotted

lathed particles
with which you lay the road
to heaven

SUFFERING AND GUILT

Only those clad in sackcloth
are able to take upon themselves
the suffering of another
to share his pain

clothed in the armorial ego
sensing the imminent moan—
we turn deaf
descrying the wound and blood—
we grow blind

we tell ourselves:
the path to Golgotha is narrow
it won't admit two people
each one must go alone

they say:
beware the suffering one
though unwillingly
he will stick you with a thorn

ON THE PASSING OF A POET

Perhaps before he died
he would reach for the shelf
where his volumes lay
as many as a few blades of grass
and tremble, the yield so insignificant
overlooked by the hasty eye

but what they left behind
after a stoic life
Spinoza's neighbours
diamond cutters
(The Hague, Amsterdam)
did it not fit barely
in the palm of a child?

SHE

In memory of Tadeusz Nowak

How she walks between us
how she observes us

sure of herself
sure of her own

as close as life
like life inseparable
(the voice suspended, silence)
sometimes she is violent
she snatches up a newborn

but she also knows how to be patient
well-disposed, indulgent
she will wait for you to finish *Hamlet*
The Brothers Karamazov, The Ninth Symphony
until you finish your tower, Mr. Eiffel Engineer

but in truth we exist
in various ways

through a note
a painting
a word

you crossed the border
towards which we all measure

Every thing that is
our strength
is also our weakness
everything carries within itself
the stigma of its opposite
like a number tattooed on a prisoner's arm
like a letter sewn onto a deportee's coat

there's no escaping it

even if we were to walk at a certain pace
head held high
number and letter warn:
here is a victim of those clothed wolf's skins
here branded by history
ecce homo

ANYWAY

Anyway
come to the meeting
there is so much to explain
we need to look each other in the eye
take on this burden
together

Anyway
don't avoid it
the most difficult task
is before us
barb and thorn
gravel of Golgotha

Anyway
let's tell each other everything
cast off the stone
and let that which has already been
breathe
its last

GOD KEEPS SILENT

God keeps silent
He allows us to think in His name
speak in His name
is but a great passivity
we're free to imagine Him

Place Him on a cloud
or draw Him a beard
cover His temples with grey hair
blacken His brow
darken His gaze

Perhaps He is a strongman
one of the eternally youthful
ready to improvise to the end
to play the most difficult games
to think up the bloodiest sports
to pull us all into them

Until tormented, wearied by the journey
through this wasteland's wrinkled skin
in a voice that roves through the cracked
corridors of the throat
we raise a shout:

God have mercy!

MAGELLAN REACHES TIERRA DEL FUEGO

They stand gazing—
                    what's on the horizon?
There it's dusk, a storm approaches
an avalanche of flashes, heaping blacks
Apocalypse in the rumble and fire

They stand gazing—
                    they wonder:
is there something beyond that spectacle?
A peaceful valley? Shaded harbour?
A path leading to a sunlit clearing?

They stand gazing—
                    they hope for paradise
and the caravel reaches the shore
and they see sand, stone and cliffs

a dead horizon

DISPATCH FROM THE OTHER WORLD

I received a letter from London:
"Linda Brendon died
peacefully and mercifully without pain."

A few days earlier we had agreed to meet in one month's time.

How happy I am, she'd said.

There was something in her eyes—
fever? anxiety?
the light of darkened mirrors?

Her skin was clammy.

Distracted
I didn't notice
she was already speaking to me
from the other world.

*

The man who
walks along the street
waits at a bus stop
stands in line
is concealed by his indistinctness
we don't know
if it is him
or someone else

whether

which

who

Everything is poetry
—Edward Stachura

1
"The swallow-tail butterfly
is yellow
with black spots and veining
on its rear wings
blue spots
on black background

the chrysalis is green

the swallow-tail butterfly
procreates twice annually
the flight of the second set of offspring
falls at the end of the summer"

2

"The mountain wag-tail
has nice plumage
a black throat-band
dark brown wings
black beak

the torrents' banks are its habitat
it calls attention with its movements
and ceaseless singing
tsissis
tsissis
tsier
tsissis"

3

"The larger bark beetle
is black or dark brown
it mates in April

the females lay eggs
from which larvæ hatch and
eat out pathways beneath the bark

young cockchafers
appear in July and
destroy fresh shoots

we find the fallen shoots
until autumn"

From Henryk Sander and Zdzisława Wójcik's *Kalendarz przyrody (Nature's Almanach)*, Wiedza Powszechna, 1983

*

To find you, the lost man
to offer you a hand, offer a word
a shred of care, a crumb of understanding
a star of perseverance
candle and flint

To find you, to say
you have in you
soil and seed
let them unite
seed will swell, will sculpt roots
you will grow a tree immune to winds

To find you, who

Will it be thus? you ask
    hand extended

BIBLICAL PARABLE

Sometimes
you behold a mote
in your brother's eye

and you watch
as it matures
as it climbs upward
as it grows into
the tree of good and evil
into a strong cedar
that Lebanese lumberjacks fell
and the Old Carpenter crafts into
a stout, evenly hewn beam
that you will carry ever after in your eye
though you do not notice it

A SOLDIER, 1975

On a plane to Luanda
a young soldier
lies on a stretcher

that morning a bullet shattered his skull

an IV hangs from a hook
the man tosses
he's delirious

perhaps he's relating what happened

we never found out
where he flew to

in the end

March trees wait for sap for leaf until a drop of
water somewhere in the earth between grains of
sand throbs swims up under the tiny beak of a
root and disappears
    Whereupon in the shade of a tree
    Adam and Eve

*

I withdrew so far from myself
that I am no longer able
to speak about myself
or what I feel
when I get wet in the rain
or when I transform myself
into a blade of dry grass
burnt by the sun
I am unable to disclose
my self
describe
its figure
name it
be certain
it exists

LAST POEMS

JANUARY 24, 2006 IN L'AMPOLLA

The clouded sky above me,
the palm-lined square before me
and farther on the gulf.
A hunched fisherman disentangles his nets.
The sea closed upon itself
silent and grey.
A waiter in the restaurant serves a round of red wine.
Empty streets.

("On the street, in the car—I note down,
so as not to forget a thing." —Czesław Miłosz)

ILLNESS

I did not want to see daylight
only darkness.
I shut my eyes
so not a single ray
would penetrate,
so I would not see
the emptiness everywhere,
from the unseen beginning
to the unseen end.

*

You'll never make up
a day you've lost,
the world went on,
you stayed behind—
your hands empty
your eyes empty.

You sit on a park bench
staring at an ant,
but even it went on.

You were left alone.

IN LIEU OF A PRAYER

I raise you on high
I raise you above the clouds
I raise you to the stars

You are so near the sun
its rays blind me
I can no longer see you

I close my eyes
darkness enfolds me
loneliness and fear engulf me

Why did I raise you up so high
that I can no longer behold you?

ACKNOWLEDGMENTS

We extend our deepest appreciation to Alicja Kapuścińska for her boundless support and for permission to translate and include four previously unpublished poems by her husband, and Iza Wojciechowska for her generosity with her time and expertise in locating two photographs from Ryszard Kapuściński's archive to accompany this volume. As well, the translators wish to thank Dan Wells and Stephen Henighan for their editorial guidance and for their faith and care in delivering a collection with which we hope the author would have been pleased.

* * *

"A Choice" and "*Ecce Homo*" appeared in *The New Yorker*.

"Yogi Ramamurti," "Tatars' Wasteland," "Sculptor from Ashanti" and "The elderly gent" appeared in *Books in Canada*.

"Tatars' Wasteland," "Barbed Wire," "Autumn in the Park," "Snow," "On Exhibit: Photographs of Polish Peasants Prior to 1944," "Lash," "The Poet Arnold Słucki on New World Street," "They" and "On the Passing of a Poet" appeared in *Exile*.

"Cudgel," "Anastasius Speaks about the Monastery," "Ravens," "Geography" and "A Conversation with J." appeared in Alphabet City's *Social Insecurity*.

PHOTO BY MAREK KUSIBA

Ryszard Kapuściński, Poland's most celebrated journalist and author, was born in 1932. His first book, *Busz po polsku* [*Bush in Polish*] appeared in 1962 and was an immediate bestseller. Many of his later works, which include *The Emperor*, *Another Day of Life*, *The Soccer War*, *Shah of Shahs*, *Imperium*, *The Shadow of the Sun* and *Travels with Herodotus*, have been translated into 31 languages and become part of the modern canon. He was, moreover, a poet, and published his poetry throughout his fifty-year writing career. One of the most acclaimed writers of our time, Kapuściński died in Warsaw in January 2007.

* * *

Diana Kuprel's translation of Zofia Nałkowska's *Medallions* was published by Northwestern University Press. She is also the editor of *idea&s: the arts & science review*.

Marek Kusiba, born in 1951 in Poland, is a journalist, broadcaster and poet living in Toronto. He has published six volumes of poetry and a concise biography of Janusz Żurakowski, *From Avro Arrow to Arrow Drive*.

COLOPHON

*I Wrote Stone: The Selected Poetry of Ryszard
Kapuściński* was designed and typeset in Adobe
Minion Pro and FF Clan Narrow by Carleton Wilson
and printed offset on 70 lb Rolland Opaque Natural
at Marquis Printing in an edition of 1000 copies.

BIBLIOASIS

EMERYVILLE, CANADA